To Amy and my family, the pillars of my life.

"Write a page a day and you'll have a novel in a year." - Dr. Jerry Thompson

Neon Noir

Jayme Lee

Amazon Kindle

The aroma of tobacco filled the dark and chilly room. Smoke from the cigar danced its way up from the ashtray while next to it, a single lamp illuminated a small corner of the papered-filled mahogany desk. The buzzing of the blue neon sign just outside the window joined the faint music emanating from the floor below. The little office had the unfortunate placement right above the stage of the bar that occupied the first floor. As rain fell upon the windowsill, the clanking of a bottle broke the stillness of the room. A man arose from his desk and joined the space around him. He was no stranger to working long hours; however, it had been a while since he had a case. So Dalton passed the time drinking whiskey, which he got on credit from Joe, the barkeep. It was at that moment at 10 p.m. when Dalton heard steps coming from the hallway outside. An ominous knock followed, rattling the door. A silhouette appeared on the frosted glass window of the door. Before Dalton could rise to answer, a note was slipped through the gold mail slot and fell onto the hardwood floor. Stillness blanketed the room once more as the silhouette faded down the hallway. The chair creaked as Dalton stood to retrieve the note. Unfolding the parchment, a sweet scent of perfume accompanied the words, "5th and Main – Dakota."

Dalton was taken aback at the unusualness of this event. He hastily opened the door to take a glance at the author of the note but found nothing in the dim hallway. As he closed the door to his office, the light outside illuminated the words "Dalton P.I." Feeling suspicious and confused, Dalton walked back to his desk with the note in hand. He knew that address yet couldn't recall the name of the place. He passed the location several times before when business was booming. It was only a few blocks down from Cider Drive, where his grungy office was located. With a quaint memory of 5th and Main, Dalton moved his focus to the strange and unfamiliar name on the note. He'd worked for ten years, and never once had he come in contact with any Dakota or ever heard of that name being mentioned. Dalton was intrigued and had no other case to work on at the moment. He gave a glance at his watch and rushed out the door, grabbing his hat and raincoat off the coat rack.

Descending the stairwell and into Joe's stockroom, Dalton opened the back door into the bar, which was filled with the sound of jazz music, lively chatter, and clinking of beer mugs. The patrons were well-dressed in suits and colorful dresses. As Dalton made his way to the front of the room, he passed the barkeep. Standing a bit tall with a white apron on, Joe was cleaning a newly washed mug as he spotted the P.I making his way out. "Another long night, Dee?"

"Yeah."

"Swell, hey, your credit is fifteen dollars. It's waiting for you." Joe uttered.

Joe was humble and a friendly man. He'd opened the bar one year before Dalton occupied the office upstairs. Their relationship was close since both men had much in common. Although they didn't serve in the war together, they connected over similar experiences. It was this fact alone that Dalton got away with late rent and a bar tab. As nice and friendly as Joe was, he was still a businessman and had to make money, especially with the way the world's economy headed.

Dalton made his way down the pouring sidewalk to the address on the note. He wasn't sure exactly who he would find when he arrived, but the memory of the location started to come back slowly. Neon lights cut the night sky from the city, exuding a glow that encircled the whole town. Every place in the town seemed to have luminous signs burning out front. Their lights were peering into apartment buildings, hotels, and just about every building in the little bayside city. Laundromats, noodle shops, radio shops, even daycares had these giant neon lights in front of them. That was why Clairsville had the nickname of Neon

City. The rain poured on, never stopping. As he approached the corner of 5th and Main, Dalton finally remembered the name of the establishment that sat on the edge.

Of course, how could he forget? The red brick building had green canopies with a dazzling sign that read, "Greens." Dalton remembered hearing about this place when he first moved to town. He thought it was a bit tacky of a place, which was named after Charlie Green. A name Dalton was familiar with since it appeared in his investigations more often than he would like. Dalton stood on the sidewalk, looking in before he entered. The private investigator had to check-in his coat and gun in by the door orderly before entering the main room per Charlie's rules. This made Dalton feel a bit uneasy, a discomfort that he hadn't felt in a long while, but it only made him feel slightly naked. Dalton glanced at his boot for a split second as the tenant checked-in his gear. A quick pat-down from the bouncer produced nothing else, so Dalton was given the go-ahead to enter. Strangeness overwhelmed him the moment he stepped inside.

How odd, he thought as the dark club appeared to be empty. Empty at this time of night? Joe's was always busy from 9:00 p.m. to about 2:00 a.m. Sometimes Joe even had to enlist the help of Dalton to clear the bar out. Confusion started to creep over Dalton's brain. It seemed that everywhere you turned in the city, you would hear about Greens. Trying to make sense of the situation, the P.I took a seat toward the back of the bar where all exits and entrances were visible. A quick glance at the place provided the necessary information that the old soldier needed to assess the situation.

As he started to sink in and settle in the green velvet chair, a waitress brought a drink, placing it on the little round table. Two men sat at the bar to the right—one was passed out. On the other side of the room was a piano player adjacent to the stage where a spotlight shined. Dalton even calculated the amount of money in the tip jar, which sat on the shiny grand piano. It struck him as odd that sixty-three dollars sat in the fishbowl of the tip jar. He gave another glance at the room; maybe he had missed thirty-some other people. Yet, a second glance proved nothing. They were still the only ones at the bar. The tension in the room finally came to an end when a voice resonated from the stage. It was angelic and immaculate, like a Siren singing on the coast, pulling him in. He had never heard anything so sweet like that before. As he locked eyes with the vixen on stage, he was drawn in by her. Soothing jazz filled the air with the somber melody wrapping around him in a warm embrace. Her ruby red lips matched her sparkling dress. It appeared as if the vixen was singing exclusively to him. When her song was over, the announcer said, "Let's give it up for Starr!" The lonely crowd's clapping echoed throughout the empty hall.

Not long after the performance as Dalton focused on his whiskey, the voice of the Siren slowly floated toward him. "Heya, Stranger," the vixen said as she gracefully made herself comfortable in the chair adjacent to him, crossing her legs and making sure her heel made contact with Dalton's leg.

With eye contact still on his drink as he took a swig of the chilled iced liquor, he uttered in a dull tone, "I'm looking for someone."

"Well, I'd say you found someone." She let out a sweet giggle.

"Is Charlie around?" Dalton retorted as he finally turned to look at the starlet vixen.

Just as soon as she heard that disgusting and bothersome name, her demeanor changed. "Oh," she let out. "Charlie doesn't come around much anymore. He's too busy with the new club up in Greensboro. He's really going hard on the green theme, how tacky. Holga runs the business in his absence." The starlet turned her head toward the side of the bar where an intimidating yet thin woman stood. In her dull grey skirt that rested below the knees, she had on a grey jacket with black lapels and a striped grey tie. Her hair pulled back so tight it started to give Dalton a headache just by looking at it. Everything about the woman's demeanor screamed power and discipline. Especially when two subordinate men walked in and made their way over to her. They both had matching dark slacks that were held up with black suspenders, which contrasted their plain white shirts. One man had a star painted on his left eye. Dalton quickly focused back on his drink before the three could glance over at their table.

"So, is your name really Starr?" he asked in a serious tone.

"It's Estrella, but I can't necessarily use my real name on stage," she retorted with seductive eyes.

"You don't have to do that; I'm not here for pleasure. I'm here on business." He tried to steer the conversation back to his unconventional investigation. What he was investigating, he wasn't entirely sure just yet. "Does anyone work here by the name of Dakota?"

The instance the name left Dalton's mouth, Starr's whole demeanor shifted once again, but not like before. No, this time, she shut down and became somewhat nervous. As if she became a whole other person. Her lips were sealed shut with a nervous twitch on the corner of her upper lip. Dalton noticed the odd behavior; he tended to see these kinds of things in his long career as a P.I.

Dalton knew he should press on, but Starr's nervousness started to transform into agitation. "I have to get back to work, Mr. Dalton. It was nice to have met you." She stood up and started to walk off when Dalton realized one thing. "How did you know my name?" he suspiciously inquired.
"Everyone knows who you are, Dee." She replied in a sweet seductive voice.

Just as quickly as their conversation had started, it appeared to have ended as the starlet walked off. Dalton's gaze fixed on her hourglass-shaped body as she slowly escaped the conversation. The look on Dalton's face wasn't one of a seduced prey, but blank, as if some memory was brought back from the deep shadows of his life. As he snapped out of his gaze, he noticed that Starr had to pass Holga at the side of the bar to reach the backstage dressing rooms. A transaction of whispers occurred between the two parties as Starr glanced back at him. Her look was a tender one, contrasting Holga's stern gaze. Her goons chuckled as they looked on to Dalton as well. It was clear that he would get no answers here, so Dalton got up and reached deep into his pockets for a few bills to pay the tab. He grabbed his coat ticket and made his way out the door. The goons exchanged words between each other, as they measured up Dalton. Finally, he was out of that strange situation and back outside in the cold night. He stood in the sidewalk facing the street for a while as the rain poured down around him. He pulled out a thin silver case from his back pocket and opened it, exposing pre-rolled cigarettes that were held in place by a flat metallic piece about half-inch wide. On the flap, the engraving read, "To my dearest love." He took out one of the cigarettes and attempted to light it in vain. The cigarette had become soaked in rainwater as the words on his case finished the memory that was started by Starr's departure.

Dalton stood there, lost in his thoughts for a while until he finally came to his senses. He shrugged at the encounter that had occurred inside the bar. The idea of not pursuing this case crossed his mind as he departed the main avenue and headed back to his office. The city around him glowed on as he walked down the street. Dalton made a stop in a little outdoor shop that had a purple neon sign that read "Ramen." He took a seat on the sidewalk stool and grabbed a menu from the bar top. A tarp canopy darted out in an angle over the patrons, diverting the rain toward the street gutters and allowing the customers to enjoy their warm soup on the sidewalk bar.

The little shop was designed so that patrons could eat and leave since people usually had places to be. As the bowl of steaming ramen came out and placed in front of Dalton, a strange feeling overcame him. A sweet scent seemed to have caught the air and passed him briefly before the aroma of the chicken broth from his noodles took over his senses. He looked around to find the source of the familiar smell but noticed nothing out of place or unusual.

Yet he couldn't kick the premonition that someone had passed by and now looked on from afar. Dalton tried to dispel the feeling, but something beckoned him from beyond the sidewalk. Just as quickly as he sat down, he finished his meal and left, leaving a tip on the countertop. The night was getting colder, so he popped his collar up to shield his neck from the wind and buried his hands deep in his pockets. Dalton rounded a corner and into an alley when an uncertain emotion bore down on him. He wasn't sure, but felt as if the moment prior to making the turn, someone had been there. The air seemed disturbed as if someone had waited in the spot, quietly observing him as he approached the alley. Dalton felt that familiar beckoning feeling again as if some unknown force was pulling him from the opposite side.

The two ends between the buildings were illuminated brightly, but the lights failed to reach the core of the alleyway. The atmosphere was charged, and the hustle and bustle of city sounds fell dead silent. Dalton could no longer hear the rain pouring down, but only the echo of footsteps as he walked. The sweet scent once again made its presence known and became more robust with each step. Dalton stood in the void of light between the two ends of the alleyway. The trail of perfume was at its strongest here, but from where did he know that scent? The sound of a match struck, as Dalton suddenly recalled where he recognized the sweet fragrance from. The note!

"Hello, Mr. Dalton," a voice said, breaking the silence of the alley.
The city streets came alive once again with the rain resuming its downpour. A woman stood with her back resting on the brick wall as she lit her cigarette. "May I offer you a cigarette? It appears yours may have gotten a bit wet." The P.I was immediately taken back by the woman. She wore a dark purple dress that ended just above her knees. It was trimmed with black lace and mostly covered by a matching coat. He noticed it looked more like a costume than it did a comfortable dress.

"You were at my office door tonight, weren't you?" Dalton questioned as the woman took a drag of her cigarette.

"Will you walk me home?" the woman inquired; she lived a few blocks from Dalton's office. It was a request that resonated with the private investigator. Of all people, he knew the dangers of the neon city. Even in a town continuously covered in light, women went missing all the time. "Dakota? Yeah, you can walk with me."

The woman smiled as she put out her cigarette on the floor, ending the life of the ember with one step of her shoe. Her high heels echoed in the alley along with the bass sound of Dalton's boots, which synchronized perfectly together like a symphony on Broadway.

"You were waiting for me?" Dalton pressed on, "Why did you want me to go to Charlie's?"

Dakota never answered his questions but only met them with a smile. The two walked in silence for a moment. The ever-present buzzing of the lights occupied the space between them.

"Mr. Dalton, you're not from around here, are you?" She stopped walking.
"Moved here after the war ten years ago," he replied.
"I'm not a neon girl, either."
Dalton started to get a bit annoyed and frustrated at the lack of answers to his inquiries. He was about to walk away from the case, leaving her standing at the corner in the pouring rain.
"Did you notice something about Charlie's tonight, Mr. Dalton? You know how busy the nightlife gets here. Don't you find it odd that the lounge was empty? It's one of the most famous land-marks in the city, curiously."

      Dalton stood fast with the realization Dakota was on to something.

"They're coming for me because I know too much, and they will get me. That is why I reached out to you; I need your help," she called to him as he tried to walk away.

Dalton stopped and stared. The air was heavy with the words

she hung out for him. Dalton was attracted to her, no doubt. The sound of her voice so soft and tender reaching out in the rain toward him. It resonated with him like a minor chord in his heartstrings. Compelled by her request, he walked back to her. "What do you know?" he inquired, this time his questions weren't left unanswered, and she finally opened up.

"My sister is missing, and I know it traces back to Charlie's. I worked there for a while to look for her. Once I started asking questions, Holga sent her goons to intimidate me. I found a book. My sister talked about secret alleyways, and there is a list of names—all of who went missing from the surrounding area." Dakota continued to impress Dalton with theories as she revealed that her sister had a secret hiding spot in a cubby backstage in the dressing room at Charlie's. "I couldn't find it, Mr. Dalton. They pretty much erased her, but it's there." She looked at him with her big eyes and her straight dark brown hair now tucked behind her ears. That look pulled him in. He hadn't said anything; he didn't have to. She knew Dalton would help her.

"It seems like you got the investigation under control. What do you need me for?" Dalton looked in her eyes as they sparkled with the city lights.

"I need you to guard my back when I find the tunnels so that I can rescue my sister."

Dalton was taken by the woman but reluctant to the plan. They both continued their journey down the street. Dalton was committed to the investigation, and he needed more information. Once they reached Dakota's apartment building, he informed her of his plan. "You probably should stay hidden for a while, especially if they're looking for you."

Dakota gave him a warm smile before planting a gentle kiss on his rough and scruffy cheek. "Good night Mr. Dalton." Her voice seductively floated into his ear. He looked on as she made her way up the stone steps and in through the glass doors to her modest eight-story brick apartment building.

Dalton turned as he reached for his cigarette case and struck a match to light it. He checked his watch for the time—it was just before midnight. Dalton started the stroll down the sidewalk, passing a street performer playing smooth, tender notes on a clarinet, his instrument case on the floor cluttered with a few bills. Dalton threw in a five-dollar coin and grabbed a flask from his coat pocket. He was lost in a forest of deep thoughts contemplating the mess he just agreed to. Dalton needed to find out anything about Charlie's, and he narrowed his research on the goons around Holga. Who were they, and how could he give them the slip? Dalton felt the only place to get answers is from a local bar where other private investigators and detectives gather late at night. Dalton turned the corner and headed down to the grungy stingy subway station. Even beneath the earth could one not escape the buzzing lights. He felt as if the walls were watching him despite the station being somewhat empty. The drunkard asleep on the bench couldn't be spying on him, but maybe the couple kissing by the platform could be. He shook the idea out of his head and played it off to his post-war paranoia. Boarding the train, he took a seat, the rattling of the tracks along with the buzzing of lights sat dully in his mind. He thought profoundly about Dakota's words. The city has a reputation for its unsolved and mysterious disappearances of the younger crowd. Still, the feeling of being watched did not fade from his mind.

When he finally departed, Dalton realized he was alone on the tram. He left the dingy underground for the fresh air of the streets and arrived at a little Victorian building with lavender wood planks and dark purple shutters. The porch had thin white wooden pillars that wrapped around the front of the building. It stood out adjacent to the surrounding buildings that were constructed of stone, brick, glass, and steel. A little wooden sign hung over the sidewalk from a pole that read "Justice." It was the local gathering place for off duty (and on duty) police personnel to gather along with private detectives and other law enforcement. He entered the bar and made his way to order a drink.

The English-styled pub was buzzing with the sounds of drunkards banging glasses together and darts hitting the board. Dalton stood at the bar, and the bartender informed him that the place served detectives who actually worked, causing the whole room to erupt in laughter. Dalton knew the joke was on him, it always was. He had himself to blame for losing the respect of these other drunkards. The memory still haunted him and drove his habit of drunkenness. It was the reason for his lack of cases. The law enforcement circuit regarded Dalton as a laughing stock—a stigma that tainted him for two years now.

It wasn't long until a shrill voice emanated from a scoundrel as he entered the bar. "Alright, first one to spill why the wasted dick is asking for...oh crap," The voice halted at the door. Dalton turned to look over at who was causing the commotion when he realized who it was. The man with the star on his face back-peddled right out the door and sprinted down the street. Dalton seized the moment to grab answers and followed. A foot chase ensured with high intensity. Dalton couldn't remember the last time he moved so fast. The man with the star was losing ground as Dalton started to catch up. They zoomed past people crowding the late-night markets and street vendors.

The goon whistled as he turned a corner with Dalton hot on his tail. As soon as Dalton turned the corner into a back alley, a thunderous sound roared in his head as if the sky cracked in two. An immense pain followed the rumbling as a force knocked the detective to the floor. Dazed and confused, Dalton drifted from consciousness. There was an abundance of darkness that wrapped around him, and the absence of light strangely comforted him. Dalton's name was then echoed by the angelic voice of a woman who was now staring at him with her hand outstretched for him to take. He knew whose voice that belonged to, and it settled his anxiety. The same memories cascaded to him as they did outside of Charlie's.

When his awareness returned, he heard two voices talking to each other. When one noticed Dalton started regaining consciousness, their footsteps shuffle away hastily. Littered with wooden fragments and pieces of plank wood, Dalton sat himself up. A storming headache throbbed his temples extensively. Dalton dusted himself off as he attempted to get his bearing. His assailants were gone with no indication of their whereabouts. The only thing left to do was head home to an ice pack and a drink. He had to keep the throbbing pain at bay. He stumbled his way out of the alley and back into the lively streets. A peddler stood on the sidewalk as Dalton emerged. "You didn't happen to catch what direction they ran off to, did you?" Dalton inquired, but the peddler only stared at his bruised face.

"Didn't think so." Dalton let out as he reached for his empty flask.

Sighing heavily with the realization he had no drink left; Dalton searched for the time as he glanced at the street clock. Its glowing green face alerted him it was 2:00 a.m. The long walk back to the office was tedious and blinding with the winding roads. Dalton focused on remaining upright. It was as if he was just another drunk making his way home. When he finally reached his office, Joe was closing up. Dalton helped, as usual, rounding up the patrons and reminding them to pay off their tabs and not to forget to tip their bartender.

"Jeez, what happened to your face," Joe greeted Dalton by pouring a scotch for the detective. Always thankful for his help clearing out the bar, the two enjoyed a drink as Dalton caught Joe up with tonight's series of events. "She sounds like a doll." Joe was just as taken with Dakota as Dalton was while he described her.

Dalton got up from the stool, informing his friend that he was done for the night. Dalton headed to the stairwell in the stockroom and up to the apartments on the third floor. His head was still pounding, and in the dark apartment, Dalton made his way to the fridge and grabbed an ice tray. Instinctively, he dropped a few cubes into a small glass, which echoed off the brown-papered walls. He then placed a few cubes into a cloth and poured himself a drink. The cooling sensation spread on his face the moment he put the towel on his forehead. With his drink in hand, Dalton made a short trip to the piano in the living room. He sat down and started to play with one finger, slowly hitting the keys in a soft and melancholy melody. Heavy was the air with the words that Dakota uttered, softly replaying over and over in Dalton's mind until he slowly drifted to sleep.

A loud banging awoke him, alarming the detective off the piano. Joe's frantic voice called out to him. Dalton jumped so quickly he failed to notice the flashing red and blue lights emanating from the windows.

"Dee, you got to come with me!" Joe called frantically as he rushed down the hallway.

Like a drone, Dalton followed, feeling confused and thirsty for answers, but Joe just hurried on down the stairs. The scurry of police officers finally got Dalton's attention as they opened the front door of the building. A small crowd had started to gather as the police hurried to form a perimeter. Dalton faintly heard a voice noting the time of death around 3:30 in the morning. Death!? What death? At the front of the building lay a body that shocked Dalton to the core. The ghastly sight vibrated through his bones, sending a shiver down his spine. Death was nothing new to him; it was a sight he regularly saw at war, but this was different. This sight shook him, and he felt the air slowly being squeezed from his lungs. He did not have the willpower to speak. The detective tried to utter a word, any word; he wanted to scream and awaken the whole damn city. He attempted to place a voice to the horror that bestowed upon his eyes, but he couldn't manifest a sound. At his feet, lay the body of a woman in a purple dress with black trim lacing. He found black heels thrown on the floor by her feet and a ribbon tied around her neck where she was strangled. The police were desperately searching in vain for her head. Strangely, the absence of blood from the body baffled the patrol officer who responded to the call, but Dalton knew this was a message. A detective with the police department approached the duo.

"Can you two identify the body?"

Before Dalton could recover from the shock and answer the detective, a voice broke from the crowd. "That's the man I saw with her in the alley. He killed her; he killed her!"

Dalton immediately turned to face his accuser. It was one of the voices he heard when he regained consciousness in the alleyway. Blinded by the glaring lights, he peered to the source of the voice. There stood the man with the star on his eye, grinning as they locked eyes. Time seemed to have dilated for the two as Dalton watched in horror as the man let out a slow maniacal laugh. The goon turned away and lit his cigarette as the police placed Dalton into handcuffs. The police car was filled with silence as Dalton rested his head on the window, which reflected the neon lights of the city. The feeling of grief overcame him. The predicament he faced would be a daunting task to overcome, but he knew he had to escape. This was no longer about finding a lost sister but solving the murder of Dakota Fleming.

AFTERWORD

Detective Dalton will return in

Neon Noir: Dying Of The Light

SPEICAL SNEAK PEAK

NEON NOIR

DYING OF THE LIGHT

Dalton stood by the stoop of the entrance when he noticed a window opened on the third floor with white curtains in the wind the wind. Something cast a dark shadow on the wall; it briefly glanced out the window and vanished before Dalton could make any sense of it.

"Thank goodness someone finally showed up. I've been calling the police department for half an hour now," a shrill voice rang out from the entrance door. A woman in a royal blue nightgown printed with pink roses and hummingbirds walked out. She had on her head a set of pink rollers as she pointed up toward the stairs just beyond the door. "A man is rummaging through that poor lady's things. I tried to stop him, but he just barreled on past me and up the steps. The damn police department keeps putting me on hold!" she called out frantically. A calming reassurance of "We'll check it out, miss," eased the woman while Dalton pulled out his pistol from his coat

The door was slightly ajar and pulsing back and forth from the breeze coming through the window. They entered the doorway and were finally greeted by nothing but a disasterous apartment room. A cool breeze entered from the window through the apartment and out the door. The curtains still flailed in the wind. A half-opened bi-folding closet door blocked the door from fully opening. The closet contents lay thrown out on the living room floor along with lampshades, lamps, papers, and clothing. The stationary was opened and emptied.

"What a hunk of mess," Dalton cried out as he holstered his

weapon. "Looks like a storm rolled through here," he added. Dalton began to pick up the lamp, placing the shade back on top of the broken bulb.

Dalton moved at a turtle's pace, trying to make sense of it all. What could they be looking for, he thought. If someone was in here before us, they must have first found whatever it is we're looking for. The curtains shifted, directtion blowing inward, and the whistling of the wind pushed around the scent of cigar and whiskey. Dalton's nostrils flared like a dog on a hunt. It was a familiar smell, and one he knew well. But this was a distinct odor he was recently acquainted with. Dalton scrunched up his eyebrows, bringing his hand off his pistol and onto his chin. The signals in his brain were getting mixed. Where did he know that scent from? Dalton tried to force the memory out into the light of consciousness. But the smell only conjured up memories of a dark alleyway. Dalton found a journal. As he opened it up he read the inner content. "East end? The docks?" Dalton wondered. The wind gusted heavily once more through the apartment when a loud crash emanated from the bi-fold closet door. Dalton instantly remembered the smell as one of Holga's goons leaped forward, snatching the journal. A blur of a figure in black slacks and a striped shirt ran down the hall. Stunned for a moment, Dalton ran out after him.

The sound of glass shattering echoed off the walls as Dalton noticed a broken vase along with shards of glass at the end of the corridor. He raced to the end, stepping on the helpless flowers that lay on the floor as he exited the window and on to the fire escape. The clanking sound of metal gave away the goon position when he jumped out and onto the street. Dalton hopped over the rail, scaling down, and gave chase. Noodles ran fast, and Dalton started to lose sight of him in the crowd. He noticed him turn the corner and into an alley between a brick building and a modern steel high-rise. Dalton dreaded turning that corner. His face still tendered, remembering precisely what happened the last time he chased one of the twins down into an alleyway. His face couldn't take another blow by a 2x4.

Dalton turned the corner; his eyes shut as he braced for what was to come—waiting for the moment when he would be bashed in the face once again. He opened his eyes to see Noodles, one of Holga's twin thugs, laying on his back, groaning in pain.

ACKNOWLEDGEMENT

First off, I wish to thank Amy, you helped me along this path and guided me each step of the way. I am very grateful for your patience. I want to thank my parents for running with my crazy idea to publish a story. It doesn't matter what crazy idea I come up with; I know I can always count on your support. To my friends and readers who helped shape the story through its drafts, you all enabled me to create a rich world from the depths of my soul. This story would not be possible without you, all my beta readers. Your feedback was essential to this project. Lastly, to Dr. Jerry Thompson, your Hemmingway class made me realize that one could be a historian and a story writer too. Most importantly, thank you for reading this story. May you get lost in this world as I have.

ABOUT THE AUTHOR

Jayme Lee

 Jayme Lee is a south Texas Native, school teacher, and local historian. He graduated with a bachelor's degree in History from Texas A&M International University in 2014. His research into a 1922 local murder and its subsequent investigation led him to write crime fiction, often utilizing real events in his stories. Jayme Lee is active in his community and established a chess club for inner-city, at-risk youth; he is also an Army Veteran.

For more books and updates
https://www.facebook.com/NeonNoirChronicles
Twitter @JaymeLeeWrites
Instagram @Jaymeleewrites

IF YOU ENJOYED THIS
CONTENT AND WOULD LIKE
TO MAKE A DONATION TO
THE ARTS PLEASE VISIT

WWW.PATREON.COM/JAYMELEE

Made in the USA
Middletown, DE
09 November 2022

14483660R00020